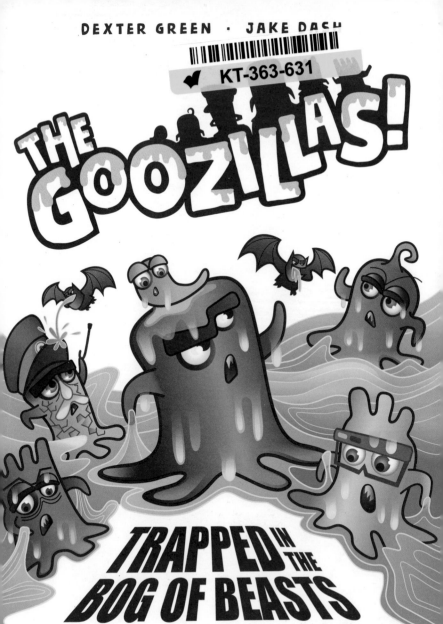

WELCOME TO THE
WORLD OF SLIME

SIX AWESOME LEVELS TO EXPLORE

Enter a team into the great **GUNGE GAMES**. There are loads of slimy sports to take part in, and win!

Leap from platform to platform, to reach the dizzying heights of the **CRUSTY CRATER**. Whatever you do, don't look down.

It's a dash to the finish line as you speed around this ultimate racing circuit. Can you reach **SLIME CENTRAL** in one piece?

Battle it out in a mission to capture the **FUNGUS FORT**. Beware: you'll need more than ninja skills to defeat the enemies on this level.

Can you escape from the **MONSTROUS MAZE**? Just when you think you're on the right track, the ghostly Gools will be ready to attack.

Dare you enter the dungeon of slime? Watch your step or you just might end up stuck in the **BOG OF BEASTS**!

CHAPTER ONE

NOSE EXPLOSION

'Eek! Look, Max! It's too cute! I'm going to burst!'

Max Rogers blew his nose into a snot-filled tissue, and tried to ignore his little sister bouncing up and down on the sofa beside him.

'Isn't it the most adorablest thing you ever saw?' Amy squealed, shoving a tablet towards Max's face.

On the screen, a fluffy pink kitten blinked its **ENORMOUS** green eyes at him and purred. 'That's Bubble Kitten!' Amy announced, tapping the screen. 'Watch!'

1

To Max's horror, the cartoon kitten pursed its lips and blew him a kiss. The kiss became a shiny pink bubble, then went **POP** against the inside of the screen.

'Ugh. Great. Now give me the tablet,' Max said, wiping his **runny nose** on the edge of his blanket. 'I want to check on my Goozillas.'

'Yuck!' spat Amy, sticking out her tongue and tucking the tablet under her arm.

'Come on, Amy, it's Max's turn,' said Mum, bustling into the room. 'You said you were going to help me bake cakes this morning.'

Amy chewed her lip, trying to decide what would be more fun. Spotting his

2

chance, Max snatched the tablet from under his sister's arm. She dived for it, hands clawing at the air.

'GIVE IT BACK!'

'You can get it later. It's my turn to—'

He stopped, feeling a sneeze building behind his nose. His nostrils tingled. His eyes watered. 'Ah . . . Ah . . .'

Nope. Nothing.

'But I want to play World of Pets!' Amy protested, but then giggled as Mum hoisted her over her shoulder and headed for the kitchen.

'Remember I installed that timer,' Mum warned. 'One hour of screen time, that's it.'

'Yeah,' Max sighed. 'I remember.'

Max headed upstairs for some peace and quiet. He closed down World of Pets and tapped the neon green icon just as he pushed open the door to his room.

A green, goo-filled volcano appeared on the screen as Max picked a path through all the toys, shoes, and dirty pants on his floor. Dozens of **slimy** figures roamed about on the volcano's six different levels, making squelchy **farting** noises as they **squidged** around.

He tapped on the lowest level of the volcano and the image changed to show a shiny gold-coloured **blob**. Tapping the magical **GOLDEN GLOB** once a day charged up the volcano's **slime** levels. If he forgot to tap it, everything would dry up and start to crumble.

But before Max could tap the **GLOB**, the tickling came again at the back of his nose.

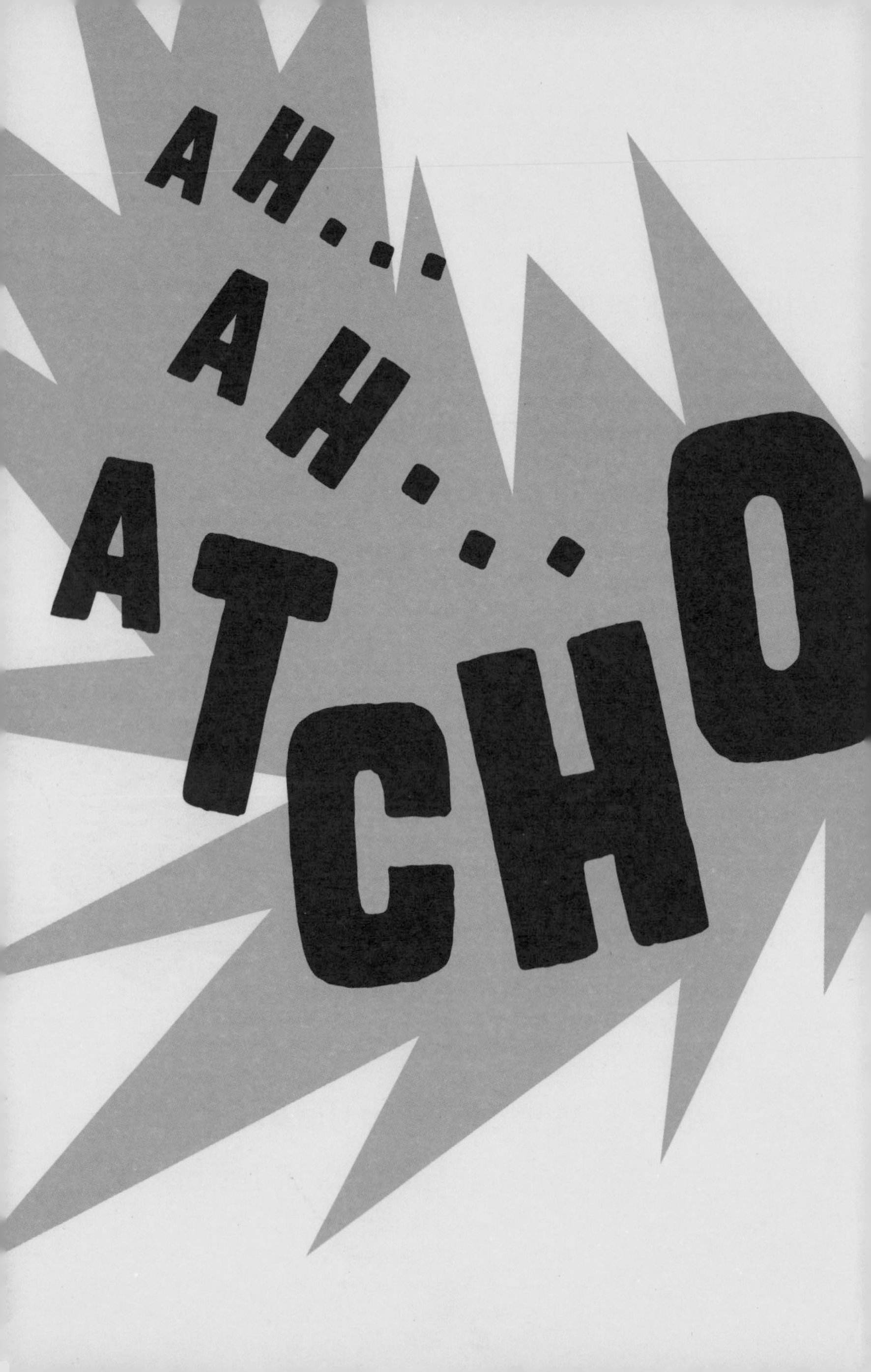

AH..
AH...
ATCHO

A fountain of nose-gunge **SPLATTERED** across the tablet's screen. The chunky blobs of bogey seemed to **FIZZLE** and **POP** on the glass.

'Whoa! Now that's a lot of snot,' Max mumbled.

His sneeze had plastered the screen from corner to corner, and something was happening to the soggy strings of snot. It was as if they were **oozing** through the glass and merging with the **gooey** graphics of the game itself.

And where was the **GOLDEN GLOB**? He was sure it had been there just a moment ago.

Max frowned.

'That's weird,' he said to himself.

The bed rippled slightly, like it was filled with water. Max let out a little yelp and grabbed for the covers, but the covers, the bed—the entire room, in fact—had started spinning like a fairground ride.

'WHOOOOOOA!' Max cried.

A bright light shone from the tablet's screen, forcing Max to close his eyes. His tummy flipped, like he was being turned inside-out and outside-in at the same time.

'WHAT'S HAAAAAAPPENING?' he yelped.

And then, with a **squelch**, the whole world changed.

CHAPTER TWO

A SLIMY SURPRISE

Max landed on something soft and **slimy**.
He stared around him in shock. He was no
longer on his bed. He was no longer in his
bedroom. In fact, as far as Max could tell,
he was no longer in his world.

Instead, he was . . . somewhere else. He
wasn't sure where, exactly, but there was
something strangely familiar about the rocky
floor, and the trickles of **gooey** green **slime**
oozing down the dark stone walls.

Was it a cave? A dungeon? It looked like it,
but there was thick white fog not too far away.
He didn't think you got fog in dungeons.

WHOO

There was a sudden roaring from beside him, like the sound of a mighty river. Max watched in wonder as an eruption of gloopy green goo exploded up out of the ground and vanished through a hole in the ceiling.

A moment later, the slime-fountain stopped just as quickly

as it had started. Max felt the soft and **slimy** thing he had landed on move beneath him. He leapt to his feet in panic. A gloopy, green **blob** stood before him, staring back.

The thing was a little shorter than Max, with two large eyes, two stubby arms, and, as far as Max could tell, no legs. **Gooey** blobs of **slime dribbled** down it, like wax on a melting candle. On its head, Max noticed, was an imprint in the shape of his bum.

The creature waggled its rubbery arms in Max's direction and narrowed its eyes. 'Stay back! I'm warning you!' the gooey figure shouted. 'I know Snot-Fu!'

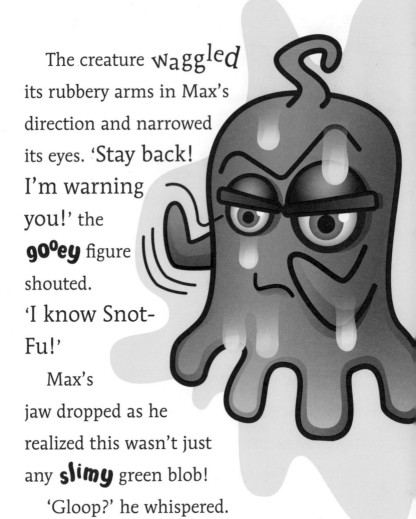

Max's jaw dropped as he realized this wasn't just any slimy green blob!

'Gloop?' he whispered.

Gloop was the first Goozilla Max had created in **WORLD OF SLIME**, and his favourite by far. Now that the bum-print was fading, the little creature looked like Gloop in every way, right down to the hooked curl on his head that let him swing across gaps on the game's platform levels.

'Who wants to know?' the **slimy** blob of goo replied.

'How is this possible? You're one of my Goozillas! I made you,' said Max. He spun on the spot, looking around him in amazement. He knew where he was, now. This was the dungeon level of **WORLD OF SLIME**. 'I made this whole place!'

Gloop's eyes widened. 'You're *The Creator?*'

Before Max could respond, something leapt out from the shadows, screeching in rage. Max jumped as a **slimy** shape hit the floor and rolled towards him. It sprung upright and took aim with a bright red weapon that looked a lot like a water pistol.

'**DON'T MOVE, BUB!**' growled an angry-looking Goozilla with one eye set slightly higher than the other. '**YOU DON'T WANT ME TO PULL THIS TRIGGER!**'

'Gunk!' Max said, recognizing the gun-toting Goozilla at once.

'You know me?' Gunk demanded, narrowing his eyes.

'Of course! You're the second-best soldier in the game!'

'SECOND BEST?'

Gunk spat.

'The lad obviously knows his onions,' said a crisp, posh-sounding voice from somewhere behind Max. He turned to find a crusty-looking Goozilla in a large purple hat shuffling towards him, leaning on a wooden cane for support.

'Captain Crust?' Max gasped.

The Goozilla's large moustache twitched. 'Indeed,' he said, tucking the cane under his arm. 'And you are . . . ?'

'He's *The Creator*,' said Gloop, his **gooey** green body shaking with excitement. 'He's the big face we see in the sky!'

'Oh, I say,' said Captain Crust, peering closely at Max. 'Yes, you do look rather familiar.'

Max stared at the Goozillas. 'This can't be real,' he muttered. 'It must be a dream. One minute I'm **sneezing** on the **GOLDEN GLOB**, the next minute I'm . . .'

A **GASP** from the Goozillas stopped him in mid-sentence.

'You destroyed the **GOLDEN GLOB**?' demanded Captain Crust, his moustache bristling.

Max blinked. 'The **GOLDEN GLOB** has been destroyed?'

18

'Or stolen,' said Gloop. 'We don't know for sure. One minute it was there, the next there was this noise like . . . like . . .'

'Like the whole world was being **SMASHED** into a hundred million little pieces,' said Gunk, glaring at Max.

'Well, it was more like a **BIG SNEEZE,**

really,' said Gloop. 'Then the next thing . . .'

'No more **GOLDEN GLOB**,' said Captain Crust. 'And, from what you tell us, it appears to be all your fault.'

'And for that,' Gunk growled, taking aim with his gun,

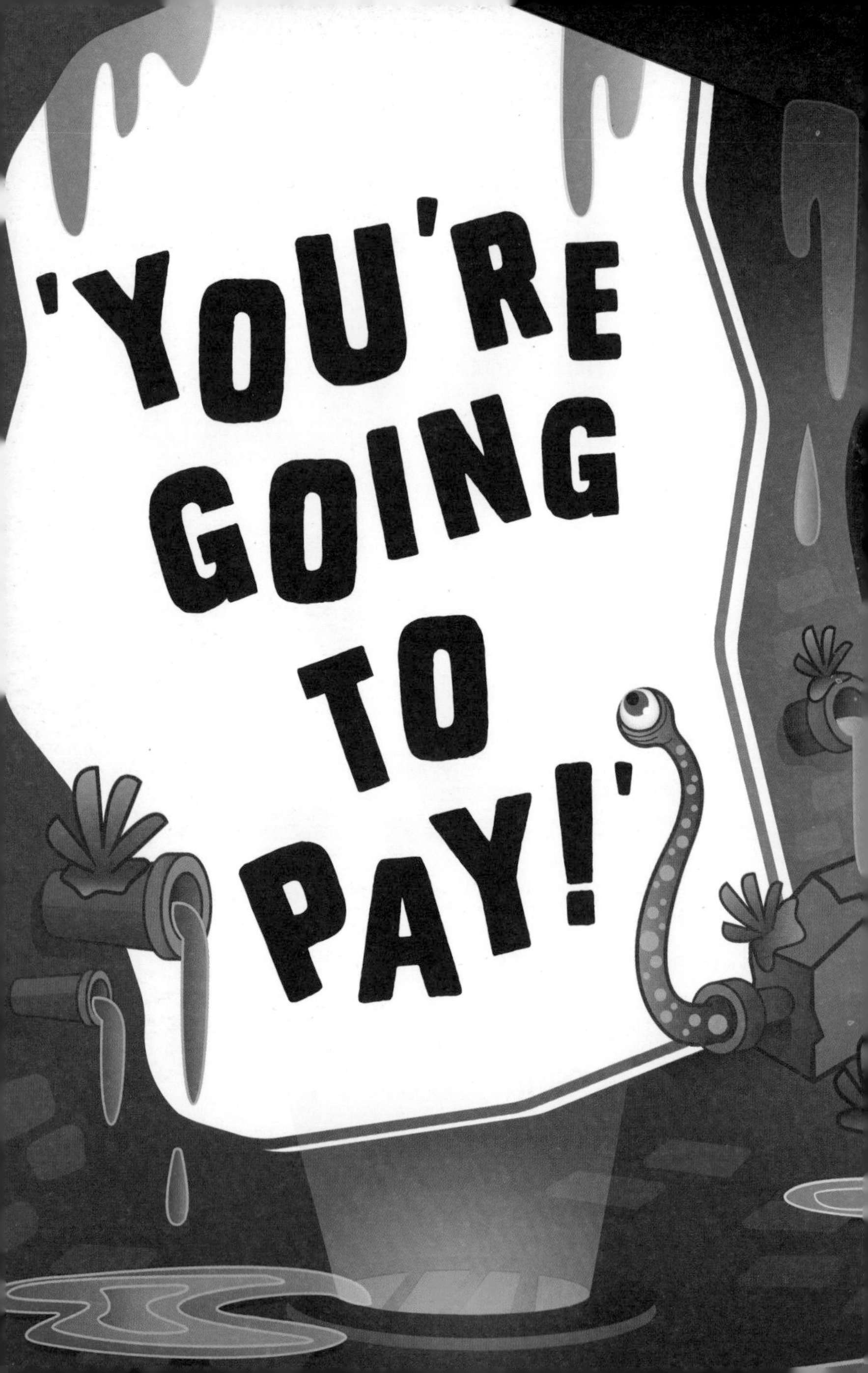
'YOU'RE GOING TO PAY!'

CHAPTER THREE

INVADERS!

'Stop, guys!' cried Gloop. He threw himself in front of Max and struck a Snot-Fu pose. 'Leave him alone. He's *The Creator*!'

'*The Destroyer*, more like,' said Captain Crust, waving his cane menacingly. 'You heard the chap; he interfered with the **GOLDEN GLOB**! That's why the **slime** is going haywire.'

'It was an accident!' Max protested.

'So you *did* do it,' growled Gunk.

He and Captain Crust advanced again. Gloop held up his hands in alarm. 'Stop!

23

He's on our side, remember? He's *always* been on our side!'

The other Goozillas hesitated. Gloop saw his chance.

'Gunk, where did you get that **Slime** blaster?' he asked.

Gunk's eyes narrowed. 'Don't remember.'

'I bought it for you!' said Max. 'The **SLUDGESPUTTER 6000**, the most powerful **Slime** gun in the whole game!'

'And you, Captain Crust,' continued Gloop, 'where did you get that moustache?'

'Good genes,' said the captain, stroking his facial **Slime** with one **gooey** hand.

'No,' said Max. 'I chose it for you. And your hat, your medals, even your **SNOTSHOOTER** cane. I picked everything.'

'See?' said Gloop. 'He's not our enemy, he's our friend! Aren't you, Creator?'

'Max. Just call me Max.'

The other Goozillas exchanged glances. Captain Crust slowly lowered his cane.

'Some friend,' Gunk growled. 'He's doomed us all!'

'I'm afraid Gunk is correct,' said Captain Crust. 'The **GOLDEN GLOB** has been destroyed. Without it, the **slime** will stop **flowing**. Indeed, the process has already begun.'

He pointed to the stone walls and ceiling. They were still **slimy**, but when Max looked closer he realized the **slime** was a little darker and crustier than usual.

'Without the **GLOB**, everything will dry out and crumble away,' said Gloop. 'Including us!'

'I didn't mean to destroy it. I just **sneezed**,' said Max. 'I **sneezed** on the **GOLDEN GLOB** and somehow ended up in here with you.'

He glanced around the shadowy dungeon. 'Where are the others? I made loads of you guys.'

'**INCOMING!**'
yelped Gloop.

He threw himself to the ground as
something small and green

WHIZZED past Max, bounced off a wall, rebounded between the floor and ceiling a few times, then landed with a **PLOP** on Gunk's head.

A tiny Goozilla, no bigger than Max's hand, blinked its little purple eyes, then smiled happily.

Gunk let out a sigh. 'Seriously, Atishoo, how come you always choose me to land on?'

'Atishoo?' said Max. He smiled. 'Hey, I've just realized my cold's gone!'

There was a **squelching** sound right behind Max.

'Hello!' said a cheerful voice. Max turned to find another Goozilla standing right behind him, smiling broadly. This one wore a pair of Gadget Glasses that had cost Max almost two hundred dung dollars back when he'd first created the character.

'Joe!' Max beamed. Joe was based on Max's best friend, who shared the same name. Like the real Joe, the **slimy** version seemed keen to become buddies.

'Pleased to meet you,' said Joe, holding out a hand for Max to shake. As soon as their hands touched, a **JOLT** shot up Max's arm, making him jump back in fright.

Joe giggled and held up his hand to reveal a practical joke buzzer.

'**GOTCHA!**' he said.

'Yeah,' Max grinned, blowing on his fingers. 'You got me.' He looked around at them all. 'What about the rest of you?'

'Most of the others don't do very much,' said Gloop.

'Or say very much,' added Joe.

'Or . . . anything at all, really,' Gloop continued. 'They just roam around the levels bumping into stuff.'

Max felt a little guilty about that. He'd made well over fifty Goozillas since he first downloaded the app. He had only spent a few seconds designing most of them, though, because it was more fun trying all the different games you could play in the World. A lot of those Goozillas didn't have personalities. Some of them didn't even have faces. 'Sorry about that,' he said.

At that moment, the floor began to shake, and Max was almost knocked off his feet as the fountain of spluttering green goo **ERUPTED** out of the floor

and up through the hole in the
ceiling again.

'That's the volcano's core,'
Gunk grunted, waving his gun towards
the tower of **goo**. 'It's supposed to
flow up through the volcano and out
through the top all the time. It keeps the
place **slimy**, and acts like a shield to
protect the whole place. But since the
GOLDEN GLOB was destroyed . . .'

The **slime** fountain shuddered,
then stopped. Drops of **goo** splattered
the ground like rain, then **dribbled**
back into the hole.

'It keeps stopping,' said Gloop.

'But you can fix it, right?' Max asked.
'You can get it flowing properly?'

'Maybe,' said Gloop. 'If we can get the **GOLDEN GLOB** back.'

Captain Crust jabbed his cane towards the hole in the ceiling.

'What in **Slime Central** is that?' he cried.

A **pink** and **sparkly** bubble had appeared through the hole and was floating down towards them.

'HALT THAT BUBBLE, BUB!' Gunk barked. **'THAT'S AN ORDER!'**

But the bubble kept coming until it touched down on the ground and then **POPPED** in a shower of little red love hearts.

A pink kitten stood before them, its wide

eyes scanning its surroundings.
Behind the cat, a furry blue puppy
with a bright red tongue wagged its
tail and spun several times on the spot.

'Hey, I know you!' said Max in surprise.
'You're Bubble Cat, from my sister's pet game.'

'It's Bubble Kitten, you fool,' the cat
corrected. For something so cute, she sounded
pretty tough. She shuddered, and a shower of
hearts shook from her whiskers. 'And don't
remind me about that game. We've seen
enough sparkly rainbows and worn enough
diamond tiaras to last a lifetime. Right, Sugar
Paws?'

The dog tilted his head to one side. 'Huh?'
he said. 'Sorry, I wasn't listening.'

Bubble Kitten sighed. 'Forget it,' she said,

wearily. She glanced around, a nasty smirk on her face. 'Nice place you've got here. A bit **slimy**, perhaps, but we can take care of that.'

'Real nice,' agreed Sugar Paws.

'So kind of you to finally let us in.'

'Very kind,' agreed Sugar Paws, nodding enthusiastically.

'WILL YOU SHUT UP?'

Bubble Kitten hissed.

Sugar Paws Puppy blinked, then mimed pulling a zip across his mouth.

'What do you mean let you in?' demanded Captain Crust. 'We didn't let you in. We don't even know who you are.'

Bubble Kitten leaned forward until she was right in the captain's face.

'WE'RE YOUR WORST NIGHTMARE!'

she hissed.

'We've been trying to escape that ridiculous rainbow-coloured prison for months. Now that your **slime** eruption has **dribbled** away, we are finally able to find our way in here.'

Bubble Kitten's green eyes blazed. Her wicked smirk became a full-blown evil grin. 'This place belongs to us now. And we're never going to leave!'

'No way!' said Max. 'We'll get the **GOLDEN GLOB** back, start the **Slime** flowing, and send you back to where you came from.'

'Ah yes, we know all about your **GLOB**,' said Bubble Kitten. 'It's what keeps this place **slimy**, isn't it? Well **NEWSFLASH, GOO-BALLS,** we don't want this place **slimy**. There are dozens of us over there in World of Pets, and we're all fed up with being made to parade around in stupid outfits. We're going to move in here, just as soon as we get rid of everything soft and sticky.'

Bubble Kitten's voice became a low hiss.

'STARTING WITH YOU LOT!'

She blew a bubble that wrapped around her and Sugar Paws, and they floated into the air. 'We'll find your **GOLDEN GLOB**,' she purred. 'And then we'll destroy it, once and for all!'

'Get back here at once!' Captain Crust ordered, but the bubble drifted off.

'Leave it to me, old man!' Gunk said. He oozed past the captain, took aim with his **SLUDGESPUTTER**, and opened fire. A jet of **oo²ing** green **slime** slammed into the side of the bubble. But instead of popping it, it just pushed it along faster.

'Uh, you do realize that's just helping them escape?' Gloop pointed out. Gunk's gun spluttered, then stopped shooting.

'Thanks for the speed boost!' Bubble Kitten laughed. She and Sugar Paws both waved as the bubble drifted off into the fog.

CHAPTER FOUR

TRACKING the GOLDEN GLOB

The Goozillas stood in a circle around Max, all shouting at once.

'This is a **disaster!**' cried Captain Crust. 'We can't have invaders just moving into the **WORLD OF SLIME**. It's not on!'

'For once, we agree on something,' Gunk said.

'What are we going to do, Max?' asked a tiny, high-pitched voice. All eyes went to Atishoo. It was the first time Max had heard the baby Goozilla speak.

'Um,' said Max. 'Why are you asking me?'

'You're *The Creator*,' said Gloop.

43

'Atishoo's right; if anyone can help us, it's
you!'

'Also, this whole thing is your fault,'
Gunk pointed out.

'Well, I don't think we should blame
Max . . .' said Captain Crust.

'Thanks,' replied Max.

'. . . Even if it is all his fault,' the captain
continued. 'Which it is. But if you can help

us, we would be in your debt.'

Max stroked his chin thoughtfully. The bowl-shaped platform where the **GOLDEN GLOB** usually sat now stood empty. The **GLOB** was what made the **slime** flow, and the **slime** was what protected the **WORLD OF SLIME** and everything in it. If they were going to get rid of the sickly-sweet invaders, they'd have to get it back.

'Joe, your glasses can track **slime** energy, can't they?'

Joe tapped a switch on the side of his specs and the glass glowed bright blue. 'Sure can!'

'Can you see where the **GOLDEN GLOB** went?'

Joe peered through his glowing lenses. A faint green trail lit up in the air. It was THIN and WISPY like smoke, but he could see it quite clearly. As he watched, five more faint lines appeared.

'OK, there's good news and bad news,' Joe announced. 'The bad news is, I can see six trails, so it looks like the **GOLDEN GLOB** was split into pieces.'

'Then we'll just have to stick them back together,' said Max.

'The other bad news is that the trails lead off in different directions,' said Joe. 'It looks like the pieces have been scattered all over the **WORLD OF SLIME**.'

'What's the good news?' asked Atishoo.

Joe shrugged. 'There isn't any. I just

thought if I said "there's bad news and more bad news" it would make everyone depressed.'

'And you were right,' said Gloop, glumly. 'What do we do now?'

The Goozillas all began talking and shouting and waving their arms, all trying to give their ideas at the same time. They were making so much noise, no one could hear what anyone else was saying.

'QUIiiiiET!'

Max shouted.

His voice echoed around the volcano. The Goozillas all stopped talking and stared at him in surprise.

'It's obvious what we have to do,' Max said. 'We gather up the pieces, and bring back the **slime**.'

'And banish that blasted kitty!' added Captain Crust. 'Why, back in my day, we didn't sit around worrying about—'

'Please, not another "back in my day" story,' Gunk groaned. He turned to Joe. 'Just tell us where the first piece is.'

Joe's usual smile was gone, replaced by a frightened expression. 'That's the *really* bad news,' he said, pointing into the fog. 'It's that way.'

Gloop gulped. Atishoo gasped. Even Gunk and Captain Crust looked worried.

'Er . . . what's that way?' enquired Max, anxiously.

48

'The heart of the dungeon,' Captain Crust replied. 'Many dangers lie along the way. **Barf Bats**. **Goo Wolves**. And, of course, the gravest danger of all.'

'A swamp, crammed with all sorts of tiny, sharp-toothed terrors,' said Joe. 'Plus a massive amount of **bogies**.'

'The bog,' Gloop said in a hushed whisper.

'THE BOG OF BEASTS!'

CHAPTER FIVE

BIG AND SCARY!

Max crept across a **slippery** stone floor, his eyes darting into the thick mist on all sides. He was in a single-file line of Goozillas, with Gloop in front of him, and Joe right behind. Gunk was at the rear of the line, his *SLUDGESPUTTER 6000* clutched in one hand. Captain Crust led from the front with Atishoo sitting on top of his hat, scanning the route ahead for danger.

In the game, the level that held the **GOLDEN GLOB** was known as The Dungeon. The Dungeon was a dark, creepy place full of **bubbling slime** pits and foggy caves.

Above the Goozillas, a group of **Barf Bats** swooped and tumbled through the mist. Max found himself looking up every few steps, in case one of them tried to dive-bomb his head.

'What was that?' whispered Gloop, his eyes darting around. 'I thought I heard something.'

Captain Crust came to an abrupt halt, and everyone else bumped into the back of him. 'Hey, watch it!' said Gunk.

'Shh!' urged the captain, putting a finger to his moustache.

They all listened.

'I just hear the bats,' whispered Max.

'No, it was like . . . a sort of **parping** sound,' said Gloop.

They all listened again, then all jumped when a high-pitched **fart** rang out right behind Max. Turning, they found Joe fiddling with a whoopee cushion. He blushed. 'Sorry. I fiddle with stuff when I'm nervous,' he said, before **trumping** all the air from the rubbery toy.

Max watched in amazement as Joe shoved the whoopee cushion inside his belly with a belchy **blurp**. 'Ew, what did you do that for?' Max asked.

'Storage, innit?' said Joe, patting his tummy.

'It's how we carry the stuff you give us,' said Gloop. 'I mean, it's not like we've got pockets.'

From behind Max, there was another **parp**. 'I thought you put that thing away, Joe!' said Captain Crust, trying hard not to lose his temper.

'I did,' Joe replied. He blushed a slightly darker shade of green. 'I also **fart** when I'm nervous. That one just snuck out. Sorry.'

'Charming,' muttered Captain Crust.

They trudged on across the soft, mossy grass. After a few more steps, Gunk let out a hiss.

'Halt!' he whispered. Max and the others stopped.

'WHAT IS IT THIS TIME?' snapped Captain Crust.

'We'll never find the piece of the **GLOB** at this rate.'

'I think we're being followed,' said Gunk, peering back in the direction they'd come from. It was hard to tell, but deep in the mist, Max thought he saw . . . a thing. He couldn't say what it was, but it was definitely a thing.

A very big thing.

And it was coming their way.

Suddenly Joe grabbed Max.

'QUICK!' Joe cried.

**'GET OUT OF HERE.
RUN FOR YOUR LIFE!'**

Max's eyes widened in panic. 'What?
Why? What is it?'

**'JUST GO, MAX!
HURRY!'** Joe yelled,

shoving him away from the approaching

creature.

Heart pounding, Max lowered his head
and began to run. He raced on, jumping
and bounding and stumbling through the

slippery grass, trying to escape the enormous shape in the fog.

'Max! Stop!' he heard Gloop shout, but his voice was now distant and muffled. Max skidded to a stop and spun around. He breathed heavily, his eyes squinting as he struggled to peer through the gloom.

'Gloop?' he whispered.

But there was no reply. Max could only see a few metres in all directions. Beyond that was nothing but misty white.

'Joe? Gunk? Anyone?' whispered Max, rooted to the spot in terror.

There was a flurry of movement, and Max was suddenly surrounded by a cloud of flapping black shapes. Hundreds of bats swarmed around him, their leathery

51

wings beating at the air. Max covered his head with his hands as several of the critters opened their mouths and hiccupped streams of hot vomit into his hair.

Barf Bats! Why did it have to be **Barf Bats**?!

Ducking, he staggered forwards, leaving the **retching** rodents behind. Somewhere, off in the distance, a wolf howled. Panicking, Max ran faster, zig-zagging past a clump of tall trees that **oozed** a **slimy** yellow **sludge** from their leaves. He was completely lost now, and felt like he was running in circles.

He dodged between some quivering mounds of jelly-like goo, slid on a slippery embankment, then stopped just before he ran into a **HUGE**, hulking shape that blocked his path.

Max looked up.

And up.

And up at the

ENORMOUS

figure towering above him.

The thing, whatever it was, had caught up.

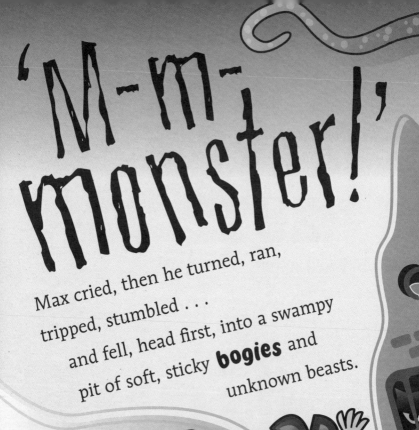

'M-m-monster!'

Max cried, then he turned, ran, tripped, stumbled . . . and fell, head first, into a swampy pit of soft, sticky **bogies** and unknown beasts.

CHAPTER SIX
SINKING FAST!

Max thrashed with his arms and legs, kicking and struggling against the warm gloopy goop. The stickiness **squelched** all around him, too soft and **slimy** to push back against. His flailing hand found a football-sized crusty chunk, but it crumbled between his fingers. He felt the scales of some unseen creature brush against his leg and then, to his horror, was aware of something nibbling at his ankle—**GROSS!** He had to get out of here!

Strands of **slimy snot** snarled around his limbs like silken spiders' webs. Bits of bogey

bigger than his head pressed in on him,
oozing him downwards into the gunky depths
and straight into the path of the beasts that
lived there.

Two thoughts popped into his head. The first
was, *Well, these trainers are probably ruined.*

The second was,

WAᴬAᴬAᴬAᴬARGH!

He could feel his breath running out. His
lungs ached. His head ached, too. Most of
him ached, actually, now that he came to
think about it. Tiny teeth were catching on
his trouser leg. The **snot** made his arms
and legs too heavy. He tried to swim, but the
gloop was too thick.

This was it, he realized. He was going to drown in the **_BOG_ OF BEASTS.**

Just when Max felt like he couldn't hold his breath for one more second, something wrapped around his ankle and heaved. This was it! One of the bog beasts had him. There would be no escape now.

But to Max's surprise, he was suddenly jerked upwards, and there was a loud SOGGY

BURP

from the bogey bog as he was yanked free of its **slimy** grip.

Hanging upside-down, Max gulped some fresh air. The monster that had chased him had one powerful hand wrapped around Max's ankle. Its **GAPING** mouth was just centimetres from Max's face.

Max was about to scream when the monster smiled at him. 'Alright?' it said in a slow, lumbering sort of voice.

'YOU'VE GOT A BOGEY ON YOU.'

'W-what?' said Max, but it came out as a high-pitched squeak of terror, so he tried again. 'What?'

'Max! Thank **oozeness** you're OK!' puffed Gloop, appearing behind the hulking brute.

Joe and Gunk arrived next. Gunk had his **slime** gun raised and was searching the fog for danger.

'CLEAR!'

Gunk announced.

The world flipped as Max was plonked, right way up, on the ground. Joe offered Max a nervous smile.

'Um, sorry about that,' he said.

Max, who was still staring up at the monster, tore his eyes away long enough to look at Joe. 'About what?'

'Telling you to run,' said Joe. 'I knew it wasn't really a monster or anything. It was just a joke.'

'But . . . but it *is* a monster!' Max pointed out. 'Look!'

'It's just Big Blob,' said Gloop with a shrug.

Max's jaw dropped. Big Blob. Of course! How could he have forgotten about him?!

Big Blob had been one of Max's earliest creations. Max had decided to build the biggest, strongest Goozilla he could, sliding his power points all the way to the top. This meant there weren't many points left over for Big Blob's brain, so although he was **super strong**, he definitely wasn't super smart.

Now that he knew he wasn't about to be eaten, Max turned to Joe. 'But I got puked on by **Barf Bats**. I nearly drowned in the **BOG OF BEASTS!**'

'Sorry,' said Joe again, looking a bit sheepish, 'I thought it would be funny to give you a fright.'

Max smiled. He couldn't help himself. It was probably just the relief of finding out Big Blob wasn't a monster, but he soon began to giggle. 'It's OK,' he said. 'I suppose it was kind of funny.' He gestured down at himself. He was caked from head to toe in chunky blobs of nose-goo. 'And now I look just like you guys!'

Joe began to chuckle, too. Then Gloop joined in, and soon all three of them were rolling on the ground, laughing hysterically.

Big Blob frowned. 'I don't get it,' he said, which only made them laugh even louder.

From somewhere in the fog there came a dry, crusty scraping sound. 'Don't panic! Help's on the way!' wheezed Captain Crust, hobbling out of the mist. Atishoo wobbled around on the captain's hat as he limped the last few steps. 'Just wanted to say . . . not to worry,' said Captain Crust, panting heavily. 'It's just Big Blob.'

'Yeah, he knows,' said Gunk.

'Ah, yes, good show,' said the captain, breathing heavily. 'Apologies. Not as fit as I used to be. You know, back in my day—'

Before he could continue, there was a loud gurgling sound, like dirty water being sucked down a drain. Everyone jumped back as the soft, shiny surface of the Bog of Beasts wobbled and wriggled like half-set jelly.

There was another sound, like the world's **BIGGEST**

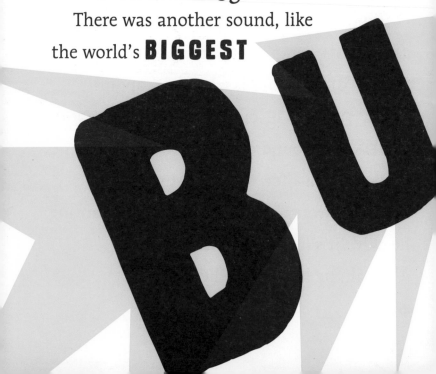

and the pit of nose-pickings turned dry and crusty.

'Uh-oh, that doesn't look good,' said Max.

'It'd be even worse if you were still in there,' replied Gloop.

Captain Crust prodded the crusty surface with his cane and punched a hole straight through it.

'GREAT GOOBALLS!'

he cried.

'It's worse than we feared. If we don't put the **GOLDEN GLOB** back together soon, this whole place will dry out.'

'Then let's go!' cried Joe, flicking the switch on his glasses that made the lenses light up. 'The first piece is this way, and . . . ah,' he hesitated.

'"Ah"? What do you mean, "ah"?' demanded Gunk, gazing into the mist.

'There's good news and bad news. But really, this time. No joke. The good news is the piece of the **GLOB** is just over there,' Joe said. 'But the bad news is someone has beaten us to it!'

CHAPTER SEVEN

THE BIGGEST BUBBLE

Max and the Goozillas crouched behind a stack of mucus blocks, peeking over the top. In the game, Max would have mined the mucus blocks and used them to decorate the volcano's walls, but right now, interior design was the least of his worries.

Big Blob had taken cover in the trees. There weren't enough mucus blocks in the pile to hide him. Max doubted there were enough mucus blocks in the entire game to hide him.

In the clearing beyond the blocks, Bubble Kitten and Sugar Paws Puppy stared at a

shiny golden fragment floating in mid-air.

'Do you think this is their **GLOB** thing?' asked Sugar Paws.

'Part of it, I think,' Bubble Kitten said. 'But I'm not sure.'

'Do you think I should lick it?' Sugar Paws asked.

Bubble Kitten pulled a disgusted face. 'Why in the world would you do that?'

The puppy shrugged his fluffy shoulders.

'Dunno. It's just what I do.'

Bubble Kitten rolled her eyes and sighed. 'Fine. If you think it will help.'

Sugar Paws didn't need to be told twice. His red tongue unrolled like a little carpet and he gave the **GLOB** a big, slobbery lick.

'Anything?' asked Bubble Kitten.

'Nope,' said Sugar Paws. He went in for another lick. 'Tasty, though.'

'That's enough!' Bubble Kitten extended a pink claw and jabbed it into the puppy's tongue. Sugar Paws yelped.

'Ow!' he said. 'Dat hurt.'

'Right. Time to destroy this thing,' said Bubble Kitten. She flicked both front paws, and the rest of her claws popped out. For the size of the paws, the claws looked enormous. They were a dark pink, and shaped like knives.

'Why?' asked Sugar Paws.

Bubble Kitten sighed. 'Because it's the only thing that can stop us, you dim-witted dolt! If those goo-balls piece their **GOLDEN GLOB** back together, the **slime** will erupt again.'

'And we don't want that?' asked Sugar Paws.

'No! If the **slime** returns they'll throw us out and we'll never be able to get back in,' Bubble Kitten explained. 'Also, I don't want to get my fur sticky.'

She raised her claws above her head. 'I'm really going to enjoy this.'

'DROP THE CLAWS, BUB!'

barked Gunk, hurling himself over the mucus blocks and taking aim with his **slime** gun. Bubble Kitten and Sugar Paws both turned. 'You heard me,' Gunk repeated, 'Drop 'em. Now!'

'They're attached to my paws, you boggle-eyed buffoon,' Bubble Kitten pointed out. 'I can't put them down.'

'Then step away from the **GOLDEN GLOB**,' commanded Captain Crust. He had his cane raised, one end pointed directly at the furry invaders. 'Or mark my words, I will **slime-blast** you so hard your head will spin!'

Max, Gloop, and Joe emerged from their hiding place. 'You don't belong in this world,' said Max. 'You should be back in **World of Pets**, sliding down **rainbows** or whatever you do.'

Bubble Kitten's eyes darkened.

'I HATE

RAINBOWS, she hissed.

'I quite
like them,'
said Sugar Paws.
'Shut up!' Bubble
Kitten snapped. She
turned back to the Goozillas,
then let out a little laugh of delight.
'Oh, come now, you don't really think you
can beat me, do you? You may outnumber us,
but even together you are no match for . . .

Hang on a minute—what in the name of all that 𝔤𝔩𝔦𝔱𝔱𝔢𝔯𝔰 is that?!'

Big Blob slithered out of the trees and stood behind the other Goozillas. Bubble Kitten and Sugar Paws both gaped up at him, their mouths hanging open.

'Alright?' he said, and the rumble of his voice made Sugar Paws Puppy's ears fold flat against his head.

'That's Big Blob,' said Max, grinning.

'He's the strongest Goozilla who ever **slimed**.'

Gloop folded his arms. 'You were saying something about us not being able to beat you?'

'STAY BACK, MAX, WE'LL HANDLE THIS!'

instructed Captain Crust.

Max watched as the Goozillas all advanced together.

Bubble Kitten slowly backed away. Sugar Paws ran round and round in little panicky circles in front of her, as if he knew he should try to protect her, but was too scared to actually do anything useful.

The piece of the **GOLDEN GLOB** was just ahead now. Bubble Kitten raised her front paws in surrender. She looked terrified. 'Fine, take it!' said Bubble Kitten. 'Please, just . . . don't hurt us. Well, me, anyway. You can do what you like to the mutt.'

Gloop reached for the **GLOB**, but then stopped. 'Huh?' he said, looking down. He was standing on a blue pawprint that could only have come from Sugar Paws Puppy's big fluffy feet.

'I'M STUCK,' Gloop realized. 'This pawprint is like glue.'

'Me too!' cried Joe.

'Blast it all, and me!' said Captain Crust.
Bubble Kitten let out a low, sinister
laugh. 'Did you really think I was going to
let you take the **GLOB**? **YOU'RE ALL STUCK.**'

'Not all of us,' squeaked the baby-sized blob on the captain's hat. Atishoo wriggled around until he faced away from Bubble Kitten. His little green face crinkled.

'AH... AH... ATCHO

Atishoo launched through the air like a missile, zooming straight for Bubble Kitten's head.

Max started to cheer, but his happiness turned to horror when Bubble Kitten pursed her lips and blew a kiss.

A bubble grew from the cat's mouth and quickly got bigger. It wrapped around Atishoo, trapping him inside. But it wasn't finished yet.

LARGER AND LARGER THE BUBBLE BECAME, GROWING AND STRETCHING

until it wasn't just big enough to hold Atishoo, but the other Goozillas, too—even Big Blob!

'Well, the good news is, the bubble has freed us from the pawprints,' Joe announced.

The bubble wobbled around on the ground for a few moments, then rose slowly into the air.

CHAPTER EIGHT

THE AMAZING FLYING FELINE

Bubble Kitty threw back her head and laughed as her bubble lifted up past the treetops.

'HA! YOU FOOLS!' she sneered.

'YOU WALKED RIGHT INTO MY TRAP.'

'Our trap,' Sugar Paws corrected, but Bubble Kitten ignored him.

'Let us out of here this instant!' ordered Captain Crust, poking at the bubble with his cane. The shiny pink sphere stretched,

but didn't pop. The other Goozillas threw
themselves at the curved sides, trying to break
free, but instead just boinged around like they
were on a bouncy castle.

'YOU CAN'T BURST MY BUBBLES!' Bubble Kitten cried.

'And with you **icky** idiots out of the way,
there'll be no one to stop us taking over the
WORLD OF SLIME.'

'I wouldn't say that!' said Max.

'Yeah! Go, Max!' Gloop cheered, his voice

echoing around inside the glittery sphere.

'Release them right now, or I'll . . . I'll . . .'

'YOU'LL DO WHAT?'

Bubble Kitten demanded.

'I . . . I . . . don't know,' Max admitted. 'But . . . well . . . I'll think of something. And when I do, you're in **BIG** trouble!'

Inside the bubble, Gunk sighed and rolled his eyes. 'Well that showed her.'

'But it'll be too late,' purred Bubble Kitten, menacingly. She pointed up at the bubble that was now rising much faster. Soon it would be completely lost in the fog. 'Only my claws are sharp enough to **POP** my bubbles. I'm sending your grubby little chums to the World of Pets. Let's see how they like playing dress-up!'

Max gazed up at the Goozillas.

Then he glared down at Bubble Kitten. She stood beside the **GOLDEN GLOB**, smirking.

'Only your claws are sharp enough, eh?' Max said, then, quick-as-a-flash, he lunged and scooped the little cat up in both hands.

'HOW DARE YOU?'

Bubble Kitten shrieked. She flicked out her claws and tried to scratch at Max's face. **'LET ME GO THIS INSTANT!'**

'Let you go?' repeated Max, dodging the claw-swipe. 'If you insist . . .' And he spun quickly back towards the bubble which was now barely visible in the clouds of white

mist. There was no time to lose. Holding
Bubble Kitten in one hand, he drew back his
arm and took aim.

'No! Don't even think
about it!' Bubble Kitten yelped.
'SUGAR PAWS, STOP HIM!'
Sugar Paws, who had been
scratching his ear with a hind
leg, and not really paying too
much attention, suddenly lumbered
forwards. But because his foot was in his
ear, he immediately fell over.

Bubble Kitten sighed. 'Oh, why do I even
bother?' she muttered, then yowled
as Max hurled her upwards into the air. Up,
up, up she flew, her paws flailing around,
just as the bubble rose out of sight.

Max held his breath as the cat vanished into the fog right behind the bubble.

One second. Two seconds. He felt his heart sink.

He'd missed.

His friends had needed him, and he'd failed.

THE GOOZILLAS

CHAPTER NINE

BRACE FOR LANDING!

Just when Max was about to give up hope, there was an almighty . . .

POP!

Max punched the air and let out a whoop of delight. He hadn't missed, after all!

With a '**WAAAAAARGH!**' Bubble Kitten fell to the ground and bounced heavily on her bottom. She looked up at Max, then let out an angry hiss.

'You may have freed your friends . . .' She picked up the piece of the **GOLDEN GLOB** and held it above her in triumph. 'But I still have your precious **GLOB** piece!'

A shadow appeared on the ground around the kitten, quickly growing larger. She glanced up to find Big Blob plummeting towards her. A look of horror came over her cute, fluffy face.

'Ooh,' she whimpered. 'This is going to—' **KERSPLAT!**

Big Blob hit the ground, his bulky body
SPLATTING down on top of Bubble
Kitten. The others rained down around him
with a series of **SPLOOTS** and
SPLOTS;

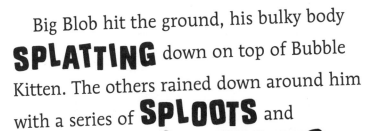

except Captain
Crust, whose
crusty hide made
a **THUD** when
he landed
on Sugar

Paws Puppy's head.
'Thanks for the
soft landing, old boy!'
the captain said,
tipping his hat to

the dazed-looking pup.

Big Blob and the others **squidged**
upright. Max half-expected to see a pancake-
shaped Bubble Kitten on the ground, but the
cat was nowhere to be seen.

'Oh no! She's escaped with the **GLOB**
piece!' said Max.

Joe grinned and prodded Big Blob's bulging
belly. 'Nah, I don't think so.'

Big Blob thrust his tummy forwards and
a **slime-covered** ball of pink fluff was
SPAT out onto the ground. Bubble Kitten's
eyes were wider than ever. Her fur was matted
with **goo**, and her mouth was pulled into a
grimace of horror. She looked like she'd just
had the worst experience of her life, and to be
fair, Max thought, she probably had.

'GAME OVER, BUB!'

Gunk said.

'We got the piece of the **GLOB**. You lost!'

Big Blob prodded his belly, making it **wobble**. If Max looked really hard, he thought he could almost make out the golden shape somewhere deep inside. 'He, he,' Big Blob chuckled. 'It tingles.'

'Pah! So what?' Bubble Kitten scowled, scooping a **blob** of **goo** off her head. 'We're still here, and we're here to stay!'

She pursed her lips and everyone jumped back. This time, though, the bubble was for her and Sugar Paws. 'You may have used me to pop that bubble, but you can't do that if we're on the inside.'

The bubble began to drift away. The evil

kitten gave Max and the Goozillas a wave. 'You may have one piece of the **GLOB**, but we'll find the others before you! You'll never stop us!'

'Hey, Big Blob,' said Gloop. 'Grab that, would you?'

Bubble Kitten's eyes widened. 'No! What are you doing?' she cried, as Big Blob reached up and caught the bubble in both hands. With a squeaky **splurge**, he tucked it under his armpit.

'Ugh, no! No! It's horrible! **LET ME OUT!**' Bubble Kitten sobbed.

'Now then,' said Captain Crust, giving his moustache a tweak. 'What say we show these two the door? Joe, can you find the exit through this blasted fog?'

Joe tapped his glasses, then peered up into the mist. 'The **slime** vent hole is that way,' he said, pointing.

'Gotcha,' mumbled Big Blob, untucking the bubble from under his armpit. His other arm began to spin. Around and around it went, building up speed.

'STOP! WHAT ARE YOU DOING?'

wailed Bubble Kitten.

'Heh, this is going to be good,' said Joe.

BADO

Big Blob slammed a powerful uppercut into the bottom of the bubble. Inside, the villains clung to each other and **SCREAMED** as they rocketed upwards through the round hole that led to the top of volcano.

Joe watched them go through his gadget glasses. 'Aaaaaand they're gone!' he announced. 'Wow, Big Blob, what a punch!'

'The **GOLDEN GLOB** must have given him a power-up,' Captain Crust said. He poked Big Blob's belly with his cane. 'Best keep that piece

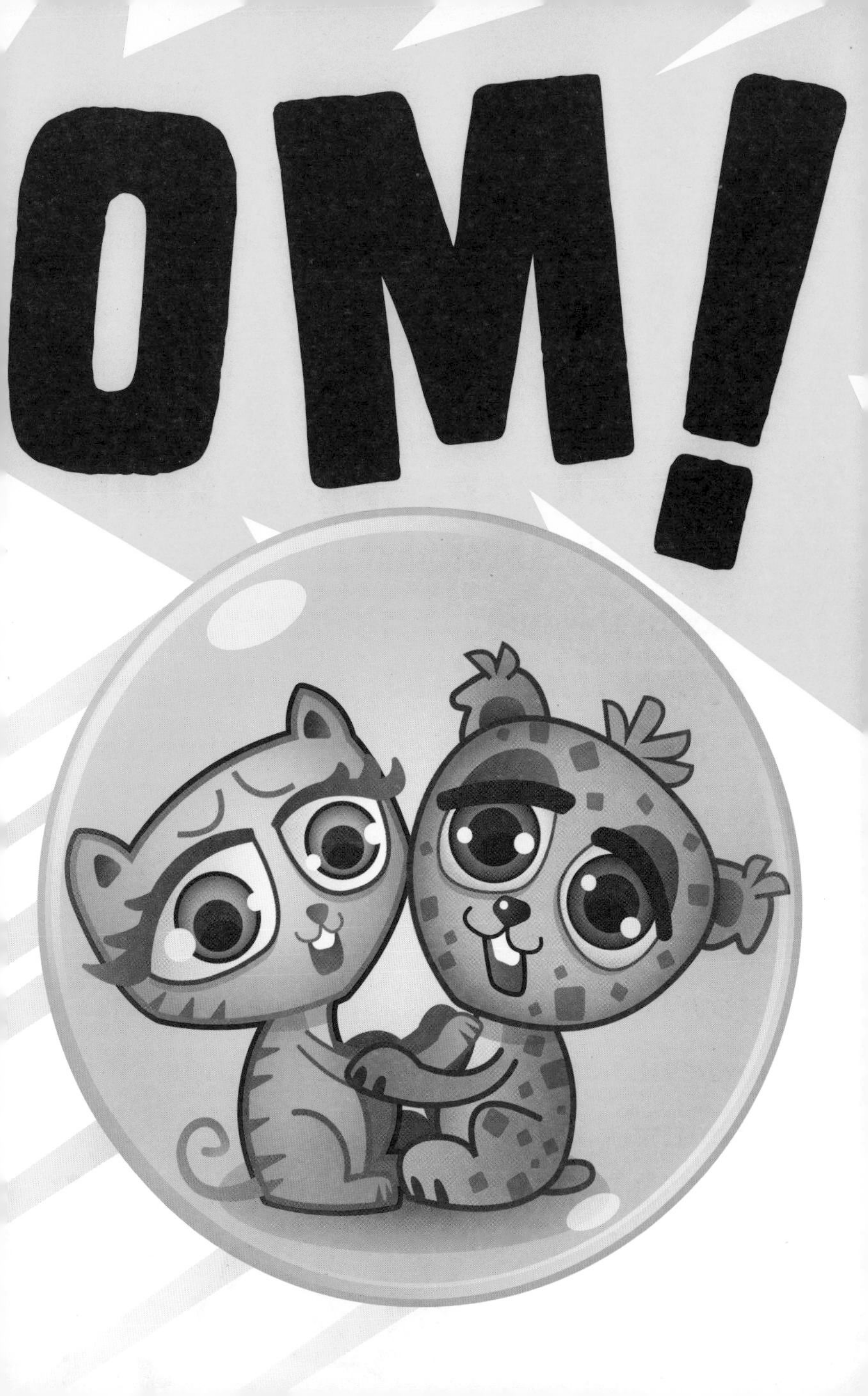
OM!

safe in there until we track down the rest.'

Max grinned. 'I guess we've seen the last of those sickly-sweet . . . Sicklies,' he said.

'Don't bet on it, bub,' Gunk said. 'I have a feeling they'll turn up again.'

BEEP-BEEP-BEEP-BEEP!

Everyone looked around as an alarm rang out across the dungeon. '**SCREEN TIME ENDING IN TEN SECONDS**,' announced a voice.

'Oh no, it's that timer Mum set up!' Max groaned. 'I have to go.'

The Goozillas gathered around him. 'But we need you,' said Joe.

'The lad's right. We couldn't have beaten those evil Sicklies without you,' said the captain.

'I totally had it all in hand,' Gunk muttered.

'**FIVE SECONDS**,' chimed the voice.

'I'll find a way back, guys, I promise!' Max said. An invisible force was tugging on him now, trying to pull him back to the real world.

'Yeah,' Gloop said, smiling broadly. 'You'd better!'

'**THREE. TWO.**'

'Bye, Max!' said Joe.

But Max was gone.

CHAPTER TEN
TEN
HOME AGAIN

Max blinked.

He was back in his bedroom. He was back on his bed. He was back, full stop.

On the tablet's screen, a message read:

Screen time over.

Come back tomorrow.

Then the **WORLD OF SLIME** app closed and Max found himself staring at all the app icons on the home screen again.

'ARGH, THAT STUPID TIMER APP!'

he groaned.

His voice came out sounding funny, and he realized his nose was blocked again.

'Brilliant!' Max cried with glee. 'I've still got the cold!'

He still had the cold, and if he still had the cold he could still **Sneeze**, and if he could still **Sneeze** then maybe— just maybe—he'd be able to return to the **WORLD OF SLIME**.

'Right, your time's up!' said Amy, charging into his room. There was chocolate icing around her mouth, and flour in her hair. 'I want to play World of Pets!'

Max handed over the tablet. 'Have fun,' he said. 'Oh, and you know that kitten you made?'

'What about her?' asked Amy, snatching the gadget from her brother.

'I think she'd look really good in a rainbow-coloured tutu,' Max said with a grin. 'And the sparkliest, most glittery tiara you've got.'

'You're right, that would look

totally adorable!

Thanks, Max!' Amy tapped the app icon, then stopped

and stared at the screen.

'Ew, what's happened to Bubble Kitten?

Is that . . . bogies in her fur?

How did that happen?'

Max giggled, then flopped down onto his bed. He tucked his hands behind his head and looked up at his ceiling. He'd been inside the game. He'd met the Goozillas! It had been the most amazing hour of his whole life.

And the best part was, Max had a feeling his adventures in the **WORLD OF SLIME** had only just begun!

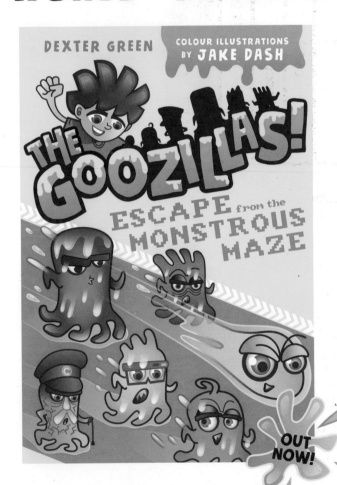